Dinosaur Hunters

written by Pam Holden
illustrated by Jim Storey

Dad gave James a telescope for his birthday.
It made everything look BIG.
"You look like a giant!" he told Dad.

Molly looked through the telescope
at the cat and the fish.
"The cat looks like a tiger!" she said.
"The fish looks like a whale!"

"Let's go hunting for dinosaurs,"
James said to Molly.
"Be very careful," said Dad.

James and Molly took the telescope, and they went outside to hunt for dinosaurs.

James looked through the telescope.
"I can see a dinosaur!" he said.
"It's in the trees. Let's go closer."
"Be careful," said Molly.

They ran to the trees to look for the dinosaur.

"Where's that dinosaur?" said Molly. "I can't see it now. It has run away. I can only see a little beetle in the grass. The dinosaur has gone!"

Molly looked through the telescope.
"I can see two dinosaurs on a hill,"
she said. "They are very big.
Let's go closer."

They ran closer, but they couldn't see the dinosaurs.
"They have gone away," said Molly. "I can only see two little lizards on a stone."

James looked through the big telescope again.
"Now I can see three dinosaurs on the rocks!" he shouted.
They went closer.
"Be very careful," said Molly.

"I can't see the dinosaurs now,"
said James.
"I can only see three turtles on
the sand. The dinosaurs have gone!
Let's go home."

At home, James said, "We saw six dinosaurs through my telescope. We went closer to look at them, but they all ran away!"